Jennifer Senne

Good Morning, Mirror

Illustrations by
Andra Moroșan

This book is dedicated to my youngest daughter, Kayla Senne. Always remember how amazing and capable you are!

Printed in China

First Printing, 2018

ISBN 978-1-7328263-0-4

JRS Leadership Development
655 Harmon Loop Rd. Ste 101
Dededo, Guam 96929

www.jennifersenne.com

I like this book because it reminds me to have positive thoughts. This book inspires me so it should inspire you too. I am giving this book 5 stars because of all the inspiration and positivity.

Kristen Manbeck, Age 9

People should read this book because it is fun, and it would teach you to think positive of yourself. It made me feel gentle and kind. It taught me to think positive of myself and everybody else.

Aspyn Nevin, Age 10

This is a cool book! It taught me to always be positive and love who I am because the way I see myself is how others will see me. I like the book very much!

Caiden Borja, Age 9

L.F. is a beautiful, smart and talented little French bulldog, and she has a friend named Mirror. Mirror and Little Frenchie grew up together. They spent so many times laughing, singing, and playing with each other.

Lately, Mirror had been acting very differently; she's been saying hurtful things and telling Little Frenchie lies about herself. Little Frenchie's mother always reminds her of how beautiful and precious she is, but sometimes Little Frenchie can't help but believe what her friend tells her.

One day, Little Frenchie was so excited to talk to Mirror; it was her first day of school, and she couldn't wait to tell her best friend. Every day when she gets out of bed, she immediately goes to her friend to greet her.

3

"Good morning, Mirror! I am going to school today, isn't it exciting?" she says with a big smile. Little Frenchie expected her friend to be excited too, but instead, Mirror spoke, "What's good with the morning? You're going to a new school, big deal! It's a big place, you don't know anyone there, and no one will talk to you. You will be on your own.

You should be scared! I know you won't have a good day, so what's good in the morning?" Mirror said with a frown. Mirror seems to be acting strangely, thought Little Frenchie. Little Frenchie's excitement vanished, and she became very nervous.

Later that day, she was lost in school, no one talked to her, and she was terrified.

She had a bad day.

Little Frenchie was very sad while sitting in what she thought was a huge, yellow school bus full of kids she did not know.
She couldn't wait to get home.
She looked out of the window, stared at her new school and thought, *"Mirror was right."*

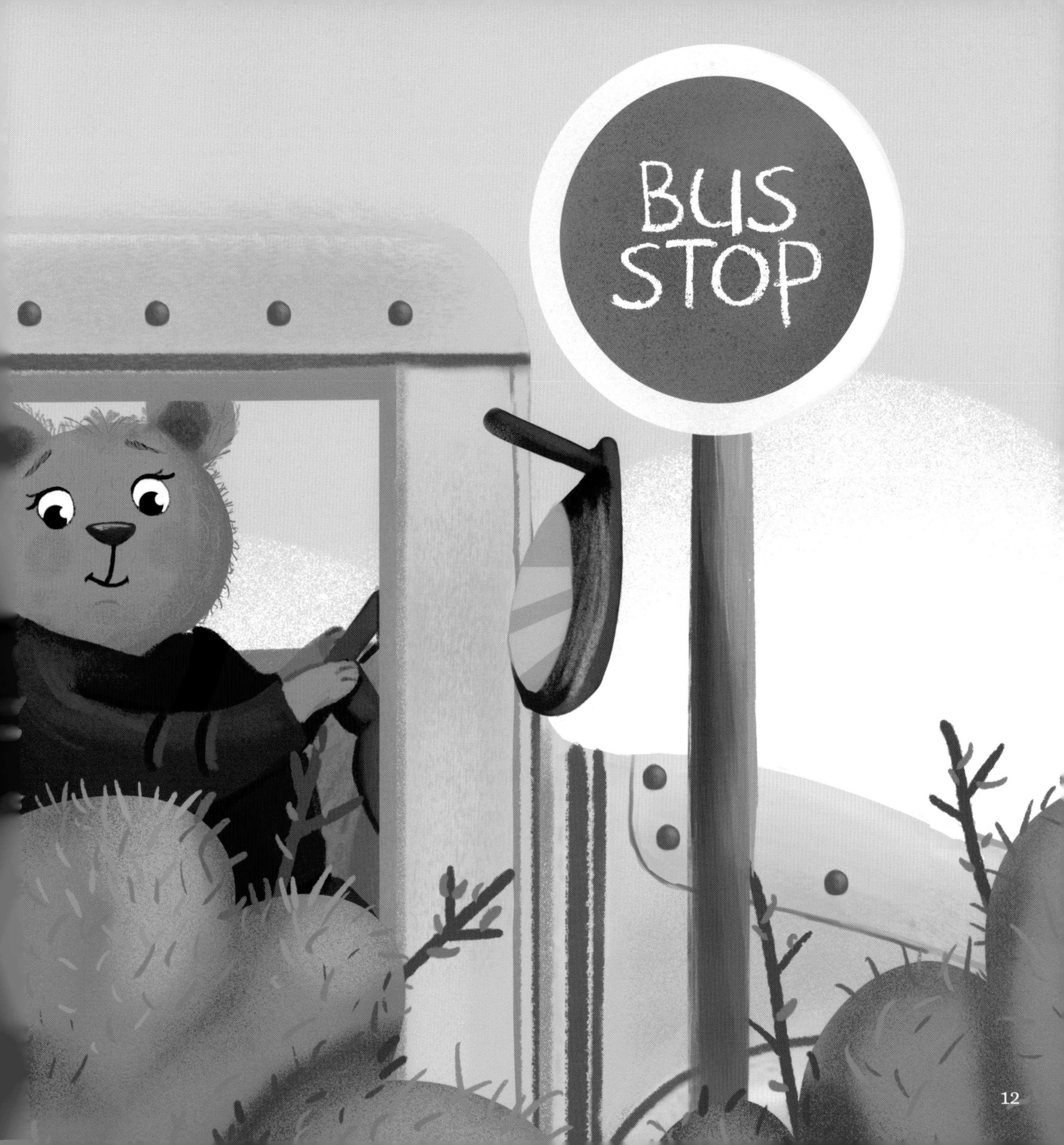
BUS
STOP

The next day, Little Frenchie's mother told her she was auditioning for the choir at church. She's been waiting for this moment for a very long time. Little Frenchie loves to sing.

Humming her favorite song, she went to Mirror to tell her the good news.

"Good morning, Mirror!" she greeted.

"What's good with the morning? I heard you're auditioning for the choir; you can't even sing. People will only laugh at you, and you probably won't make it anyway!" Mirror replied with a scowl on her face.

"But, we used to sing together, and I thought we were good singers." Little Frenchie explained.

"Nah, many other kids at church can sing better than you. What makes you think they will pick you? You are not good enough."

Little Frenchie stopped humming and walked away. She was very sad.

Later that morning at the audition, she was so worried about what Mirror had said that she could not sing at all. Instead, she decided not to go through with it.

"I am not good enough, what was I thinking?" Little Frenchie told herself while listening to the other girls singing. She felt sorry for herself, so she decided to walk away. Little Frenchie had a bad day.

Later that week, she was invited to a birthday party. She was very excited! She grabbed her favorite dress to show it to Mirror, "Good morning, Mirror!" she happily greeted her.

"What's good with the morning?" replied Mirror. "Going to a party?"

"Yes, I am!" answered Little Frenchie.

"Why? Your dress is so old and ugly; the girls will probably make fun of you. You don't belong with those girls; they are prettier and more popular than you. Since you will not have a good time, what's good with the morning?" asked Mirror.

Little Frenchie was hurt by what Mirror had said. She stared at her favorite dress and threw it on the floor. With tears in her eyes, she looked back at Mirror and said, "You're mean!"

She could not believe her best friend had turned against her. She jumped into bed and cried. Momma saw her pup was crying, "Tell me what's wrong little one." Little Frenchie sat up and told Momma what Mirror had said. Momma quickly realized what was going on.

"Look, my Little Pup, what Mirror had told you is not true. C'mon let me show you."

21

They both got up and looked in the mirror.

"Tell me what you see," Little Frenchie's mother asked.

"I see you and me," replied Little Frenchie.

"That's right! Now, what about me?" asked Momma.

22

"I like your dress, you look tall, and you're pretty!" Little Frenchie answered with a smile. Momma beamed at her little Pup and said,
"Thank you! Now tell me what you see in you."

Little Frenchie looked down, sad.

"Now c'mon, look at yourself in the mirror and tell me what you see."

"I see me," said Little Frenchie.

"That's right! What do you see in you, my love?"

She looked in the mirror and saw that she looked so much like her Momma. "I look like you, Momma!" she announced enthusiastically.

"You sure do, my child. Do you think you're pretty?" Little Frenchie hesitated for a bit and finally said, "Yes?"

"Of course you are! I think I'm pretty, and if you look like me, then you should think you're pretty too!" her mother teased. "See, whatever you think about yourself is what Mirror sees, and sometimes Mirror will tell you negative things about you. It's because that's how you feel about yourself," her mother explained.

"You mean, I have control over what Mirror tells me?" She was a little confused.

"Yes, you do! A mirror can either be your friend or your enemy. It's up to you what it should be. Why don't you try having her as a friend? This time, think positive thoughts."

Little Frenchie gave it a try and looked at her friend, Mirror. She thought of something positive about herself and hesitantly said, "Good morning, Mirror!"

"Good morning, Little Frenchie," Greeted Mirror back with a beaming face.
"You sure look glowing and pretty today!"
tle Frenchie was surprised by her friend's response.
"Wow, I did not know that how I feel inside is what Mirror will tell me!
I have to do is think positively!" Little Frenchie was very excited to
cover the truth.
"Thank you, Momma!"

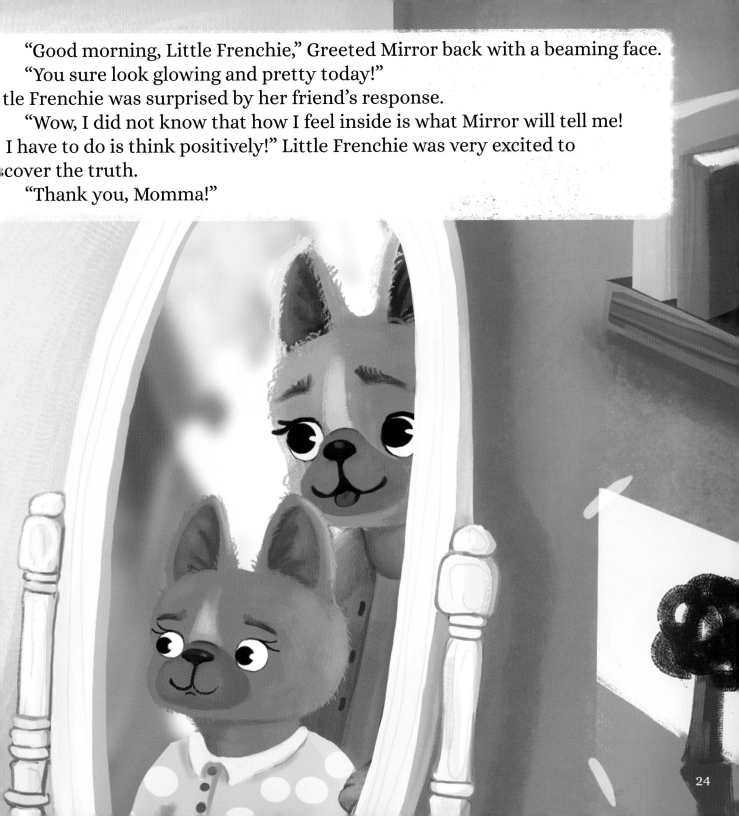

24

The next day, Little Frenchie was so excited to talk to her friend again. This time she remembered what Momma said.

"Think positive," she whispered.

She paused for a while, stared at her reflection, took a deep breath; and said, "Good morning, Mirror!"

She waited for Mirror to greet her back and finally, Mirror replied,

"Good morning, Little Frenchie, you look beautiful today!"

Little Frenchie was so happy by her friend's reaction, "…and I love your dress too! Do you have plans today?" Mirror asked with such interest.

"Yes, I do! I am going to school this morning, go to my audition this afternoon and spend time with my new friends after." She eagerly shared her plans with her friend.

"Wow, exciting day! School is fun, and you will enjoy your time there! I'm glad you decided to give the audition another try. I believe in you, my friend, so sing your heart out at the audition. You will do well, and I know you will get the part!" Mirror announced.

"By the way, have lots of fun with your new friends, I'm sure they will love you. I can't wait to meet them!"

"Wow, thank you, Mirror!" Little Frenchie was so thrilled to see her best friend back!

"I love you, Mirror," she whispered.

"I love you too, Little Frenchie! Remember, love yourself and always stay positive no matter what!"

And that's exactly how Little Frenchie's day turned out to be; a beautiful, meaningful positive day!

I wrote this book not only to encourage others but to encourage myself continually. See, I am Little Frenchie - well not really, but I am very much like her. Most of the time, I know how special I am, but there are times when I look in the mirror and see just the opposite. I start believing all the negative things I tell myself and when I do, my days usually end up awful. As a child, I had low self-esteem - stopped by all the self - limiting beliefs I had imposed on myself, and this carried throughout my adult years. It took me years to realize how valuable I am as a person and in the meantime, had passed many opportunities in life. I am hoping that this book will encourage children to guard their self-talk, to believe, and to be kind to themselves. I think that the earlier we expose our children to how beautiful, capable and amazing they are, the better person they will become. When they know how valuable they are, they are more likely to add value to themselves, others and become successful in the future.

To the children who think they are not good enough, guard your self–talk; always stay positive. Remember, a mirror can be a friend; tell her or him some encouraging words daily and she or he will respond with some encouraging words for you. When others try to bring you down, remember it is ultimately your choice whether to believe them or not. Be strong and believe in yourself. I hope you learn something from this book and may it help you add value to yourself and the people around you!

Believing in you,
Jenn